WARNING

This book contains sexually explicit scenes and adult language. It may be considered offensive to some readers. This book is for sale to adults ONLY.

* * * * * * * * * * * * * * * *

Please store your files wisely where they cannot be accessed by underage readers.

ISBN-13: 978-1987863888
ISBN-10: 1987863887

Other Books by Darla Dunbar:

<u>The Romeo Alpha BBW Paranormal Shifter Romance Series</u>

Amanda Walker thinks that she has a normal and boring life. That is until after her 24th birthday. Everything changes when she meets the man who says he was supposed to be her husband. Denying everything the man says, she fights him every step of the way. But after he kidnaps her, Amanda discovers that there are some things about her family that her parents kept a secret all these years. Among the history of the family she learns secrets she thought only happened in story books. Can Amanda tell the difference between truth and lies or is she this mysterious woman that holds the key to a legacy?

<u>Romeo Alpha Blood Lines Romance Series</u>

Twenty-four years have passed in relative peace for Amanda and Romeo. They've raised five children into adulthood and are thoroughly enjoying their lives as the Alpha King and Queen of the werewolves. At twenty-four, Sarina is just stepping into her powers and will be ripe for mating when her birthday comes in two weeks. What no one knows is the danger that lurks just outside their tight knit community. Romeo has made peace with the other clans and has enjoyed that peace, but it will all come crashing down around him when his oldest daughter comes of age to take a mate.

The Alpha Feud BBW Paranormal Shifter Romance Series

Eliza's life consisted of reporting on boring, crowd-pleasing events, like their country livestock fair. With the arrival of two handsome brothers, the lives of Eliza and her best friend, Melissa, are shaken to the core. For Eliza, the arrival of this new man becomes a test of her relationship with her current boyfriend, who she's been happily living with for over six years. Does Hayden, a complete stranger, really wield the power to make Eliza reconsider her relationship with Andrew?

The Alpha Packed BBW Paranormal Shifter Romance Series

Darlene has led a quiet life since suffering through a terrible break-up. She wants nothing more than to spend her time in front of the TV, away from any sort of trouble. But all that goes down the drain when handsome, rugged and rough Idris comes into her life. He is a werewolf on the lookout for his missing pack leader. Darlene quickly finds herself pulled towards this mysterious man and at the same time finds herself falling deeper and deeper into the world of the supernatural.

The Mind Talker Paranormal Romance Series

Ananda finds herself on the run and she's not alone. With help from Jared, a stranger that she just met, the two evade capture by an organization that is intent on hunting her kind. Ananda and Jared are able to read minds. When an unfortunate incident happened involving a disturbed individual that resulted in the death of his schoolmates, the secret organization decided to take action.

<u>The Leather Satchel Paranormal Romance Series</u>

Valtina is stuck in Middle World, unable to pass on to The Afterlife. In order to redeem herself from past deeds done, she must help bring romance back into the world and stop The Dark Side from destroying love in its entirety. Following orders issued by Ladaya and armed with a leather satchel filled with the appropriate tools and weapons, Valtina embraces each mission with enthusiasm.

Get the latest update on new releases from the author at:

https://darladunbar.com/newsletter/

This book is Part Six of "<u>The Daemon Paranormal</u> <u>Romance Chronicles</u>"

Book 1 - The Awakening

Phoebe grew up not knowing her mother. The stranger, Apollo Mikos, claimed to know her mother. After that day, Phoebe's life would change forever.

Book 2 - The Shifter

Phoebe is surprised when her dog, Ace, shows up from nowhere. She is on a mission with Apollo to kill the Qilin. That is the only way that the true leader of daemons will emerge.

Book 3 - Forgotten

Juno has been stirring up trouble that has prolonged the infighting among the daemons. In order to get her to stop, Phoebe agrees to give up a year of her memories. But making deals with a siren is never a good thing. Without her memories, Phoebe's romantic relationship with Supay no longer exists. Instead, she leaves Supay for Apollo.

Book 4 - The Siren's Trap

The unsuspecting couple, Phoebe and Supay, made a deal with Juno to stop the infighting among the daemons. But at what price? An entire year was wiped clean from Phoebe's mind. Now Phoebe was with Apollo. Desperate to get her back, Supay considers Juno's new deal. Is it worth the price to pay for the dubious result? To win back Phoebe's love, Supay will need to be unfaithful to her.

Book 5 - Exposed

Hiding away in Peru, Supay and Phoebe start their own family, away from the chaos and the daemon infighting. Meanwhile, Apollo, heart-broken and lost, is lured into another one of Juno's schemes. Making deals with a siren never turns out right. If Apollo accepts the deal, the love of his life may resent him for the rest of his natural life. If he doesn't take the deal, she is lost to him forever.

Book 6 - The Beginning

As preparations for the war between daemons are underway, everyone must begin to choose. Siding temporarily with Apollo, Juno has a moment to look back on her life and figure out how she arrived at this moment. As she sifts through memories of the past, a specific dark stranger stands out. How far will young Juno go with her new love? More importantly, will her mother, Circe, discover the secret tryst?

Book 7 - The Treachery

Having broken the cardinal rule of the sirens, Juno must take action to save her own life and the life of her unborn child. In order to keep her secret safe from the sisterhood, she must kill her lover and conceal her shame. Will Juno betray the sisterhood and save her lover or will she remain loyal by slaying him instead?

Book 8 - Duplicity

Juno's mother, Circe, discovers her lies and gives her an ultimatum to fix everything. As Juno races against the clock to protect her loved ones from Circe, she makes a final choice that could leave her perpetually unhappy. Left to wander the world alone, Juno realizes that freedom means nothing if there is no one to share it with. The nature of Juno's vendetta—and the means she achieves it with—are finally revealed.

Book 9 - Reconnaissance

As Juno's hunt for the daemon's fortress unfolds, Apollo is left alone wondering if she will truly return to him. Will Juno be able to resist her base instincts? More importantly, will she be able to get to the fortress and return without being spotted? Discover how Juno's stealth mission works out.

Book 10 - The Interrogation

Juno tries to hide her rising fear in the presence of her captors. As her fear mounts, she holds on to the hope that Phoebe or Supay will take pity on her. Before that can happen, she has to come clean to Supay about her past. Could he possibly forgive her for what she has done? Will Juno remain faithful to Apollo or will her siren urges take over? Discover how the confrontation with Supay unfolds.

The Daemon Paranormal Romance Chronicles

The Beginning

Book Six

By Darla Dunbar

Copyright Revelry Publishing 2015

Table of Contents

Chapter One

THE CALL of an archer could be heard on the battlement. Juno snorted. It wasn't really by choice that she was here with the Romans. Unlike other daemons, she had no allegiance. Although the majority of sirens were part of the Greek tribe of daemons, sirens were not creatures that claimed allegiance to everything. She had, unfortunately, ended up here because of outside circumstances.

Not long ago, she had created a careful plan to wreck the life of Phoebe Williams. At the time, she had hoped that it would bring Supay back to her. That had never materialized and she had instead been left with Apollo. Like her, he had been left without a daemon tribe. After her last attempt at breaking Supay and Phoebe apart, Apollo had been left to suffer from the fall out. He had hoped that Phoebe would choose him in the end. When she had not, he had thrown all of his efforts behind the Roman tribe. They were a rough and tumble bunch, but he no longer seemed to care. Instead, Apollo had quickly developed a singular focus on revenge. Juno had thrown her lot in with Apollo out of the hope that something would jar Supay out of his sickeningly complacent relationship with Phoebe.

Gazing back at the archers, Juno just shook her head. The slight tilt of her chin caused her straight black hair to sway back and forth. Her overly large eyes narrowed uncharacteristically as she tried to hide her annoyance at the Romans. For some reason, they seemed to think that this daemon war was a medieval battlefield. Over the last few months, they had started building supplies and weapons at this lonely base in Sicily. Since she had sworn to stay out of the fight due to her agreement with Phoebe, Juno could not step in and show them how they were doing it wrong. For starters, they had placed the archers on the lowest wall. As the easiest location to climb, the lowest wall would be better suited to giant vats of tar and boulders. Other than a complete lack of knowledge in this field, the Romans also lacked the ability to see that they would be easily routed. Although modern weapons and techniques drew more public attention to the daemon wars, they were also more effective.

Sniffing disdainfully, Juno went back into the castle. She may have promised not to actively fight, but that didn't mean that she could not remain up-to-date on the latest happenings in the daemon world. Purposefully navigating the corridors of the castle, she began to climb the narrow stairs that led to the north tower. With its poorly made steps and drafty interior, few people bothered to enter this part of the castle. This one fact made it perfect for her use.

Entering the tower, Juno set about closing the curtains. At the last curtain, she stopped and peered out at the ground. Below her, Apollo was shouting orders as he tried to get the troops in line. As she watched him, Juno felt a stirring of something within her heart. Not long ago, she had convinced Apollo to sleep with her.

Although he had been appalled at the idea when she asked, he had readily returned to her bed since that time. Juno sighed. The life of a siren was never easy. Long ago, she had planned out a different, beautiful life for herself. Since that time, everything had gone wrong and now she was just another siren operating in a chaotic world.

Approaching the sink, she filled several pitchers with water. Each time one pitcher filled, she brought it to the table and used it to fill up a scrying basin. Circular and sleek, the ebony marble gleamed in the evening light. In just a few moments, she would use it to gaze across the world to watch the enemy at work.

Sitting at the table, Juno began to focus her mind. The clutter of her thoughts would not quiet readily, so she leaned back with a sigh. If she could not watch the Greeks mount an attack or Supay attempt to stop the battle, she should do something else. Her mind wandered as she thought about what she needed. After all this time, she had allotted very few moments to herself. Her rosebud lips pursed slightly before relaxing into a grin. Yes, this was just the time for her to revisit her past. A reminder of how she arrived at this place in life would be just the thing that she needed to renew her focus. Settling into the chair further, she waved her hand confidently across the water of the scrying tub. As the ripples expanded outward, pictures began to reveal themselves.

Chapter Two

Across the field, a young, beautiful girl darted among the sheep. The dappled sunlight on the ground jostled merrily as the leaves moved in time with each gust of the breeze. Gorgeous and strangely innocent, the young girl fell next to the herd of sheep after a stray rock tripped her up. Laughing prettily, she shook out her straight black hair from a messy bun. The raven black hair fell neatly on her back as she gently combed her fingers through it. Gazing out at the sheep, young Juno knew that there were few better places to be in the world.

Each morning, she picked up her crook and a loaf of bread before heading out toward the Andes. Over recent years, her tribe of sirens had settled down in the area. Known for causing trouble, they never stayed anywhere for more than five or ten years. This time, Juno wanted them to stay. She loved waking up to the smell of coffee brewing and wandering the fields with her sheep. Her mother, Circe, had given her this task to keep her out of trouble. Until her nineteenth birthday, Juno was an untrained siren. Unfamiliar with the ways of the world or sirens, she was told to keep herself out of mischief. As a shepherdess, it would be next to impossible to get into trouble. Honestly, Juno preferred her life this way. None of the sirens like her Aunt

Pasiphae or her mother were ever happy. They pretended to be happy and were certainly charming, but the siren way of life tended to be a lonely one. Men were taken and used, but never kept, and love was forbidden. According to her mother, it was impossible for a siren to ever become anything else.

Leaning back into the sweet meadow grass, Juno relaxed luxuriously on her arms. The noonday sun beat above her head and reminded her that it was time for lunch. Rolling over, she reached for her pack and pulled out the loaf of bread. It would be eaten with a small jug of milk. She sighed and her dainty eyelashes drooped slightly. The jug of milk was leaking again. Today would be another day that she would go home starving.

Just as Juno was about to begin her lunch, she heard a noise at the far end of the meadow. Some of her sheep were darting out of the way, as strange sheep approached. Standing up quickly, Juno dropped the loaf of bread on the ground. Cursing at her stupidity, she leaned down to pick it up. With her intent focus on cleaning the bread, she almost forgot about the strange sheep. She glanced up just in time to see a large, black dog dart into view. It seemed intent on herding the sheep into the meadow until it caught sight of her. The sudden shock of seeing someone else caused the dog to lose focus. Before Juno's eyes, the black canine transformed into the naked form of a young man.

Her almond eyes opened widely. "Sir...?" she asked curiously.

Groaning in embarrassment, the young man reached around for something to cover himself with. Juno realized his shame and smiled. Unwrapping the shawl around her waist, she tossed it over to him. Grinning bashfully, the young man tied it around his waist and walked over.

He reached out his hand. "Hi, I'm Supay. I... well. I apologize. This doesn't normally happen. Surprises still jolt me out of shape shifting. I'm still learning. What's your name?"

Juno smiled prettily and stretched out her thin, delicate hand. "I'm Juno. Don't worry about your mistake. I think you're the first person I've seen up here in months and the first man I've seen at all in years."

Supay tilted his head. "What do you mean? How could you not see a man for years?"

Sitting down, Juno picked up her bread again and offered him a piece. Supay began to eat before Juno started speaking again. "Well, it just happens that way. I have to be secluded during the last few years before my apprenticeship or I would get into terrible amounts of trouble. That's why I'm up here herding sheep." She glanced over at him. "I'm sorry to ask, but are you a daemon? I didn't realize boys could be daemons."

Staring at her in disbelief, Supay just shook his head. "You never knew there were male daemons? What are you?"

"A siren." Her large eyes watched him innocently. On hearing that she was a siren, Supay choked on his bread.

"You're a siren? You don't seem like one."

Juno frowned. "Well, I'm not exactly one yet. I don't start training until I'm nineteen. After a year of training, I will officially be a siren."

Supay took a swig of her milk jug and thought for a minute. "So if you don't do training, would you stay like this forever?"

"I don't know, I suppose so. I have to be a siren. All of my family becomes sirens and that's what I will be one day as well. Besides, what's wrong with sirens? Basically everyone I know is a siren."

Glancing at her, Supay tried to figure out a way to explain the concept of a siren to her without offending her. "Well," he paused. "Sirens are not really known for being nice. For the most part, they are just good at charming or tricking other people. I have never met one until you, but my brother warned me to stay away from them."

Juno grinned. "From me? How silly. What's your brother like?" She reached for a piece of bread and began nibbling at it without paying attention.

"Well, he's quite nice actually. And honest. So I'm sure he's right about how other sirens behave. Yossele is only a few years older than me, but he's seen a lot more of the world." He took another bite of the bread. "Yossele's a golem."

"A gol… a gol-what?"

"A golem. Like you're a siren, I'm a shape shifter and he is a golem. It's not a particularly good daemon to be. Basically, he's super strong and can call spirits back from the dead. It would be great if he could just do those things, but that isn't all. As a golem, he can be controlled by someone else."

Fascinated, Juno leaned closer to Supay. Only inches away from him, she could smell the scent of prairie flowers on his skin. If she shifted just slightly, she may be able to see what was behind the shawl around his waist.

Frowning at her momentary distraction, Juno focused on what Supay was saying again. "So, you could control your brother?" she asked.

Supay frowned. "I could, but it would be a bad choice. In the past, some golems have gone insane and started murdering everyone they came across. My father believes that this was due to the golem following orders that it didn't believe in. He thinks it creates a kind of psychological break from reality for a golem—or anyone, really—to be forced to do something that they don't believe in. Yossele has lived far longer than the average golem because we intentionally protect him from having to follow an order." Supay patted his chest. Realizing he wasn't wearing a shirt, he grinned. "Well, if I had my shirt on, I could show you. I keep the incantation that controls him with me. Only my father and I have those incantations. We keep them around in case someone else tries to take control. Those incantations are the only way for us to bring him back."

Juno wanted to meet his brother. She couldn't imagine such an unusual family. Despite her interest in his story, she was still struggling to remain focused. The rippling of muscles on his arms was enticing and she was using all of her strength to avoid running her hand upon his body. "So, has anyone tried to take him?"

Shaking his head, Supay reached down to adjust the shawl. Next time, he would have to bring clothes. "No, we've never had a problem so far. If someone did control him and Yossele went out of control, there is a specific part of his mouth that I press. It's a neural pressure point on golems that cause them to stop."

Leaning back on the meadow grass, Juno tried to take it all in. In one day, she had met a fellow daemon who happened to be a shape shifter. She had learned about a crazy new type of daemon known as a golem. Juno rolled over to face Supay. To her surprise, he was still looking at her. When he realized that she had caught him staring, he looked away bashfully. "I'm sorry. You're just so beautiful."

Juno lowered her eyelashes demurely. She wasn't sure how to proceed. Until her training, she would not be taught how to entice, charm or trap a man. Yet, she already had the opportunity to learn right in front of her—and she was ready to learn. Reaching her hand out, she ran her tiny fingers along the muscles of his arm. Beneath the gentle press of her hand, his biceps moved reflexively. Glancing up at her, Supay recognized the same desire he felt. There was something else in her eyes, however. A type of caution or innocence that he had seldom seen in a young woman her age.

Reaching out his hand, Supay ran his finger through her long black hair. Beneath his touch, Juno trembled like a leaf. The sudden realization of what her behavior meant dawned on Supay in a split second and he pulled his hand back. "You've never been with a man, have you?" he asked, although he already knew the answer.

Juno shook her head and leaned toward him conspiratorially. Raising her hand up to her curvaceous breasts, she slowly pulled at a string on her bodice. Nervously, she watched him as she pulled the string completely out. Without the tight laces holding her breasts in, they bounced out readily. In the chilly mountain air, her nipples hardened into small pink centers within seconds. As she drew up her courage to look at Supay's face again, Juno quickly realized that she didn't need to fear his reaction. In front of her, Supay sat frozen as if he were mesmerized. Her innocence and beauty had washed away any thought that did not involve her.

Smiling, Juno leaned forward to kiss him. The closeness of her sweet figure jarred Supay into movement and he pulled her into him. Wrapping his arms around her waist, he tilted his head and ran his tongue along her lips. The sudden sensation excited Juno and made her want more. Without knowing what she was doing, she pressed herself against him. All she knew was that she wanted to be as close to his body as possible.

Supay ran his fingers across the nape of her neck. The delicateness of her collar bone excited him and spurred him onward. Running his hand downward, he felt the sudden, sweet plumpness of her breasts. He played with her nipples gently as he began to kiss along her neckline. Her body enticed him onward. As he drew closer to her, he could smell the scent of jasmine and lavender rising from her body. Unable to resist, he pulled the top of her bodice down with both hands.

Surprised, Juno instinctively went to cover herself. Before she could, Supay stopped her. "There's no reason to cover such beauty." He paused. "Is this okay? Do you want me to stop?"

Shaking her head, Juno looped her arms around his neck and pulled him closer again. She reached down with one hand to untie the shawl from around his waist. Looking down, she saw his cock barely constrained. With an instinctive knowledge of how to please him, she worked her hand quickly along his member until he could barely control himself. Fascinated and turned on, she watched as he came to the brink of orgasm over and over again. Unable to take it any longer, he pushed her hand away.

Shoving her onto the grass, he placed himself in between her legs. For a moment, he was unable to enter her and he realized that her tightness would make it impossible. Groaning in frustration, he controlled his desire long enough to whisper a word of warning in her ear. "This is going to hurt, I'm sorry."

With one thrust, he pushed himself violently into her body. The tightness and wetness he encountered drove him mad. Driving deeper and deeper inside her, Supay struggled to stave off orgasm. He wanted her to orgasm for her first time, but was uncertain if he would be able to hold off long enough.

Juno tilted her hips upward to meet his. After the first few moments of pain, the pleasure had increased rapidly. Within her, there was a deep longing to have him within her forever. Pushing her hips against his, she enticed him to enter her deeper and deeper. With each thrust, she could feel a tremendous, dangerous feeling beginning within her body. Unaccustomed to such pleasure, it took her several seconds to realize that she was about to orgasm. As the first rolling waves of her orgasm hit, she tightened her legs around his body and pulled him into her. Unable to hold off any longer, Supay came with her.

Long moments passed as the pair lay in the meadow grass. The late afternoon sun beat down on their sweaty bodies. With pleasure, Juno tilted her hips up to his again. Despite her exhaustion, she still felt the urge to continue. In answer, Supay thrust once again into her body before he withdrew.

Lying back, Supay glanced up at the sun. "We both will have to leave soon. I don't want to leave you, but we can meet here again tomorrow. Would that be all right? And was your first time good enough?"

Juno smiled. The warm afterglow that filled her body had not yet receded. "Yes, yes to all of your questions. Tomorrow, we will meet again." She glanced over at him again. "That wasn't your first time, was it?" she asked curiously.

Supay shook his head. "No, there was a time in mid-school, but really I haven't dated very many girls. I guess I'm as new to this as you." He kissed her forehead.

Juno nodded. This entire day was perfection. Tomorrow, it would all begin again.

Chapter Three

Sitting at the kitchen table one night, young Juno watched her mother cook dinner. Things were happening in the world of daemons, but Juno was too young to be included in the discussions. After another day spent with Supay, Juno was exhausted and infinitely happy. As a child, she had read stories of princes arriving to sweep women off their feet. She had never believed in true love until she met Supay. From the moment they were first together, everything had seemed like a marvelously happy dream. Even when she was away from him, she spent her time humming and singing with joy.

Glancing over at Circe, Juno cleared her throat. Her mother finished pulling out a tray of pita bread before looking over at her. Shyly, Juno started to talk. "So, mother. I was wondering... when do I start my training?"

Circe smiled. "I told you, not until you are nineteen. You'll grow up soon enough." Pulling off the oven mitts, she placed some hummus next to the pita bread and started to eat.

Juno picked up a piece of pita. "And I'm not allowed to learn about men or being a siren or the outside world until then?"

Finishing her bite of pita and hummus, Circe paused as she tried to think about how to respond. "Look, dear, it's not just my rules. It's how sirens have always done it. You have an innate skill to charm men and entice others into doing your bidding. Until you are old enough to harness that skill, you should not stray too far away from us. The amount of trouble you could cause in the outside world is truly unthinkable." Seeing her daughter's sad expression, Circe held Juno's face up to meet her eyes. "Sweetheart, trust me, it's for the best."

Not wanting to betray her relationship with Supay, Juno tried to figure out what to say. "Um... but in books, girls my age always find a soul mate or a boyfriend. Why can't I?"

Shaking her head, Circe frowned. "You don't want a boyfriend. Sirens don't fall in love or have boyfriends. Unless you want to be out on your own, you will avoid men until your training is over." Picking up the plate of pita, Circe turned to the sink and began to clean up.

Judging by her mother's behavior, Juno knew the conversation was over. A slight flicker of light caught her eye from behind the barn. Supay had remembered to arrive for their secret meeting. With his ability to shape shift into faster creatures, it was easier for her to steal a moment to meet him here. Juno looked over at her mother. "I'm going to put away the sheep and chickens for the night, mother." Not waiting to hear a response, she ran out to the barn.

In keeping with her excuse, she began to put the sheep and chickens away. As she started to toss hay down from the loft, she was tackled by the figure of Supay. Smiling, she looked over at him. "You found the clothes!" She grinned. "It's almost too bad I left those for you. You looked so much better naked."

In response, Supay pulled her body against his. He kissed her passionately as he grabbed her by the hands. Pulling her into the darkness of the loft, he sat her on his knee. Not waiting for a response, he slid his hand up her dress and ran his fingers along the inside of her thigh. Moaning slightly, Juno kissed him gently. "Shh... you'll have to be quiet. I kind of asked mother about you. There's no way I could ever introduce you until after my training. Even then, you could never be introduced as the man I love." Hearing those words, Supay stopped rubbing her thigh. Unable to believe his good fortune, he held her chin face up to his.

"The man you love?" he whispered. Unable to find her voice, Juno just nodded. Kissing her passionately, Supay pulled her legs over his so that she straddled him. "I love you, Juno." Holding her against his chest, he ran his fingers along the small of her back. "Let's not talk of your family now. We'll worry about them later. For the moment, I just want to enjoy the fact that I am loved by the most beautiful woman in the world." Hearing this, Juno smiled again. The longer she was with him, the less she was able to worry about her family or their expectations of her. She just wanted to be with him.

Pulling her dress up to her waist, she readjusted herself on his body. She could feel his hardness beneath the jeans. No longer just a sweet virgin, Juno knew that she wanted her lover in her immediately. Pulling at his pants impatiently, she ripped one of the buttons off. It rolled into a corner as she stripped his clothes off of him. Resuming her position above him, she pressed her body onto his and began to rock her hips. After several weeks apart, it was impossible for her to hold back her desires. They had to be satiated and fulfilled before her longing consumed her.

Behind his head, she grabbed two of the handholds that protruded from the walls of the loft. Pulling against them with all her might, she used the handholds as leverage to push her body further onto his. The angle of his hips caused her clit to tingle with anticipation. She wanted more than this. Every minute of every day, she needed to be with him like this.

Beneath her, Supay groaned with pleasure. The frantic movements of Juno had urged him on to the next level. Grasping her breasts with his hands, he thrust his member fully inside of her. Unsatisfied with just that, he grabbed her hips and pulled her roughly against him. Her slender body was easily manipulated as he thrust his way into her. Faster and faster they moved in perfect rhythm until their bodies were pushed to the very limit of human endurance. Crying out in pleasure and agony, Supay and Juno orgasmed as one being.

They fell together onto the floor of the loft, breathing heavily in synchronicity. With the pleasure of orgasm already passing, Juno did not want to think of what would happen next. Supay's daemon family had expectations similar to her own. While she had to work in the background until she came of age, Supay had to alternate jobs in the family business. First, he worked as a shepherd. Over the last few weeks, he had started to work in the family's copper mine. Although his family was more open to different ideas than hers, it still meant that she would not be able to see him for several weeks. Kissing his hand gently, she let her face rest on his chest. "Until next time, *mi amor*," she whispered.

Chapter Four

Juno was becoming increasingly nervous.
Something was wrong with her, but she was afraid to
tell her mother. Perhaps she had too much sex? Or the
longing for Supay had started to take its toll on her
body? If Supay were here, she would discuss the matter
with him. Unfortunately, it was still another week until
she would see him again. After meeting him in the loft,
he had managed to leave a message at their meadow.
According to the message, his family would not be
leaving the mines for at least another three months.
Apparently, copper prices were up and every worker
was needed to increase production.

Already, it had been two months. Juno had an entire
month to wait to see him again and figure out the
strange disease that was harming her body. Sitting in
her window seat, Juno tried to enjoy her view of the
Andes. It was impossible. She literally had no clue what
was wrong with her. Without paying attention, she
rubbed at her belly. Over the past month, a bump had
started to form and grow larger. Accustomed to the
ways of the siren, Juno had never been told what to
expect with a pregnancy or how to prevent it. The entire
siren upbringing was focused on keeping the young
sirens away from the world. As adults, sirens would
leave the familial property to find mates, earn their way

in the world and have children. The morning sickness and growing belly were a mystery to Juno that she was anxious to solve.

Walking over to her closet, she tried to find something to wear. As a wave of nausea washed over her, she tossed one shirt aside after another. There were very few clothes left that would hide the changes in her body. If her mystery illness was somehow connected to Supay, she must do her best to hide it. Unfortunately, she had been increasingly tired lately and the few oversized shirts that she possessed still needed to be washed. Sighing, she finally settled on a sweatshirt over her skirt. The sweatshirt was tight, but it had the thickest material of any of her remaining clothes.

Exiting her room, Juno slowly started to walk down the stairs. If she was lucky, she would be able to sneak out the back door and leave with the sheep. It did not always work, but it helped her to avoid suspicion. Her mother loved using feta in everything and just the thought of eating feta cheese disgusted her.

One step away from the bottom of the staircase, a loud creak gave Juno's position away. In the kitchen, her mother glanced up. "Juno, come get your breakfast. You hardly eat in the mornings anymore, darling."

Wincing, Juno started to step softly into the kitchen. Struggling to keep her belly behind the counters, she sat down as her mom began serving up breakfast. Mumbling her thanks, Juno began to take a bite before she realized belatedly that her mother had used too much feta again. Retching immediately, she dashed to the sink and threw up the contents of her stomach. As her heaving subsided, she turned back to face the room instinctively. For the first time in weeks, Circe was able to see her daughter in full profile.

Circe raised an eyebrow. Beneath the dulcet tones of her voice, Juno could hear the rage that was barely controlled. "What... have... you... done?!" Livid, Circe waited for Juno's response. When nothing happened, Circe threw a plate against the wall. It shattered into a thousand pieces with a resounding crash. Glancing back at the quivering form of her daughter, Circe stepped forward. In quick succession, she threw each plate around Juno's figure so that they barely missed her body. Struggling to avoid being hit, Juno winced as dishware crashed around her. The desire to run away was only beaten by the fear that running would increase her mother's anger.

When no dishes remained in the room, Circe sat down again. With a restrained calmness that scared Juno more than her mother's anger ever did, Circe swept the pieces of the dishware off the table with a cool flick of her wrist. Looking at Juno again, she motioned to the chair. "Sit. We will fix this."

-To be continued in Book 7-

If you enjoyed this title, I would appreciate your leaving a review of the book. Good reviews encourage an author to write as well as help books to sell. Good reviews can be just a few short sentences describing what you liked about the book without having a spoiler.

If you could spend 30 seconds writing a review, I would appreciate it: you can review this title right now at your favorite retailer.

Here is a preview of the **next story** you may enjoy:

THE SOUND of footsteps jarred Juno out of the darkness of her memories. With her mind refocused, she realized she was back within the castle in Sicily. She gazed around, confused and tried to spot the source of the interruption. Amid the gloomy shadows of the tower door stood Apollo. Juno hid the confusion and annoyance on her face.

Juno needed to fix her mess before she could walk over to Apollo,. Moments prior, she used the scrying bowl to review images of her past. Now, she acted to hide any evidence. Although her memories were not confidential in any way, she did not want him to see some of her most painful recollections. She pulled a pinch of sand from her pouch and sprinkled it over the magical bowl. With a wave of her hand, she whispered, "*Finite.*" The replay of her past disappeared from the surface of the water.

With her most seductive face, Juno slinked toward Apollo, sexier than the best of sirens. "What brings you here, my darling? Weren't you preparing the archers?" Juno circled his figure and leaned in to run her teeth down the edge of his ear. Biting lightly, she pulled away.

It did not matter how much time he and Juno spent together. Her scent still affected him in an intoxicating way. A hint of jasmine washed over his senses; he struggled to keep his face from responding to her physicality. Juno was more than a woman to him. She was a temptation and the physical embodiment of sensuality. He may be repulsed by her actions, but he could not control himself when he was around her body.

Apollo tried to act nonchalant as he steadied his voice.

"There's no point in helping the archers. They are positioned on the wrong side of the castle. Invaders will be able to surmount the wall with little effort while the boiling tar is placed above a wall that is too high for it to ever be needed."

Juno smiled. A few hours earlier, she was thinking the same thought. Perhaps Apollo was smarter than he appeared. "I agree. What brings you to my lonely tower, my sweet?" She smiled. Even in the darkness, Juno saw Apollo watching her figure with hunger in his eyes. With slow deliberate strides, she allowed her hips to sway hypnotically. In one fluid motion, she sat down upon the settee. In a nonchalant manner, she shifted her skirt from her legs so Apollo could see the full length of her calves and thighs.

Apollo skulked toward her, feeling like the entire world stopped revolving around the poles. In its place, the new pole shifted to this very room. Nothing changed or moved in the tower while life revolved at its own pace in the world outside. In his chest, his heart beat ever faster as he cursed his lack of control. Before him sat the last woman he wanted to be with, but the only person he was physically mated to. He wondered absentmindedly what Juno did before he arrived. He opened his mouth to ask, but forgot his question as he caught her scent again. He gazed down her full body. "I... wanted to see you again," he said.

Those words gave Juno much pleasure. "Well, here I am." She leaned back along the couch and ran her fingers down the side of her neck. At the center of her bosom, she pulled on two strings that held her peasant blouse together. Her outer garment fell open to reveal a dark purple camisole that attempted to hide her nipples beneath them.

Unable to resist any longer, Apollo spread his legs across her body and pinned her to the settee. Without waiting to ask, he ripped her shirt into two pieces with one hand. Her camisole still hid her breasts from his view. Apollo glanced up at Juno as he reached for the straps of the camisole. He pushed the straps down her shoulders and allowed her breasts to break free from the constraints of clothing.

Apollo glanced up at her face and caught a fleeting glance that unnerved him. Unguarded for a brief second in time, her glance appeared almost loving or caring. Before the exact nature of her expression registered itself in his mind, Juno smiled and the moment evaporated. While ignoring this thought for the moment, Apollo lowered his head to her breast and began to lick her nipples. Her round, firm breasts were malleable beneath his giant hands. Ravenous and unsatisfied, Apollo knew he needed her. He also knew he would never stop needing her like this. Each curve of her body tempted him into a never-ending game of seduction.

Beneath his fondling, Juno moaned. Distracted by her memories, she did not realize how much she needed him until this moment. Her legs spread, she forced him between her thighs. With her skirt pulled up, he caught sight of the gentle slope of her thighs and the soft mound between that welcomed him. He could no longer hold back. His head tingled with anticipation as it delved into her wetness. A low guttural moan escaped from within as he thrust his entire shaft into her.

Juno arched her back as she received the satisfaction she needed. Slight whimpers of desire rose from her lips as she urged him on. Her legs wrapped tightly around his form, she pushed her hips against his. The rocking and insatiable desire that emanated from her body only turned Apollo on more. He needed this. If this moment lasted forever, it would be his version of heaven. He thrust into her body deeper; she moaned and dug her nails deeply into his back. The sudden pain served as a catalyst for him and brought him closer to orgasm. Beneath his body, Juno's body started to clench as orgasm approached. With their urges taking over, the couple came as one in a fit of ecstasy. In her mind, Juno floated away from the memories, the doubts and the stresses of the day. The only thing that existed was the body of Apollo and the sensation of him inside of her.

Juno moved Apollo's body off hers as the bright, vivid sensation of orgasm waned from her mind, . His spent figure draped like a Greek god across the settee. Juno stepped away to admire Apollo's form. Long, lean muscles stretched taut across his chest and arms. His golden hair was tousled from their recent exertion and his weary eyes followed Juno. The daily preparations for the daemon war took their toll on him. Juno smiled at him. In the last few months, she grew close to Apollo. Without realizing it, she even started developing feelings for him. She tried to hide it, but her emotions remained. With a sigh, Juno turned away. For sirens, having feelings was never a good idea. Without thinking about it, she rubbed the tip of her nipple as she stood above him. Only her skirt remained on. Her shirt was ruined, but it did not bother her. She would take Apollo's button-up shirt later.

Juno looked back at Apollo. He would be asleep in a few moments, but she did not feel like waiting. She slid her fingers over his eyelids and muttered a quiet incantation. In seconds, Apollo fell asleep.

Juno wandered over to the scrying basin again and waved her hand across the surface of the water. In moments, the memories of her past appeared.

Her mother, Circe, sat in front of Juno. The cold anger in her eyes remained barely hidden as she demanded the name of her lover. Young Juno winced. She may be naive, but she never doubted her mother's ability to kill. Death would be the least terrible thing a full-fledged siren could do to Supay. Juno tried to think about what to do as her mother coolly asked for the man's name again.

If you enjoyed this sample then look for **The Treachery - The Daemon Paranormal Romance Chronicles, Book 7.**

Here is a preview of **another story** you may enjoy:

Unfaithful - The Leather Satchel Paranormal Romance Series, Book 2

EVEN THOUGH Valtina had had a great time helping Joshua and Samantha, she was having a hard time accepting the fact that her job was not yet over. After all, it was very difficult to go from thinking she was on her way to The Afterlife as a reward for finishing her job to the realization that she'd only just barely completed the first task in a list of many. She stood there, trying to come to terms with the idea that she still had a long way to go.

"So… am I really the only one who can do this job? Am I the only person you have?"

"Valtina, there are many people who can help me work with these couples, but you are by far the best at what you do. Don't think that you are the only soul at work right now. Currently, I have at least a dozen others on Earth completing their own missions. That is not your concern right now. The better you help each of these couples, the more the universe will improve and the sooner you can continue on to The Afterlife. For now, though, I need your help."

Valtina paused for a moment, wondering if she really wanted to ask her next question. She did anyway, saying, "Okay Ladaya… But just how many people are we talking about? How many more couples do I have to help along?"

"Right now, I am not sure. The Dark Side is currently working against us and they are gaining power quickly. Every day, they bring more and more people over to their side. Now, it is a matter of how many of these people we can save. We need to bring as many souls back to the light as possible, otherwise we will lose this battle forever."

Clearly, this was a very serious task. This put a great deal of pressure on Valtina and the other souls at work. "I'm going to give you some of the hardest tasks, because I know that you will be able to complete them. I will not ever give you any jobs that I don't think that you can complete. In love, you are the best person that we have."

Ladaya smiled kindly at Valtina, trying desperately to convince her. For a few minutes, Valtina mulled over her options, or at least tried to. It didn't take her long to realize that she had only one other option. However, she didn't want to be reincarnated again. After living countless lives in various bodies and time periods and situations, she was tired of all of the work and monotony. She sighed heavily, "Alright Ladaya, where do you want me to go next?"

"Next, I have a couple that is the perfect example of what will become of the world if The Dark Side wins. They feed off of misery, despair and lust. Each couple that they drag over is living in a great deal of unhappiness. Matt and Amy are the next couple that you will work with. They have been together since they were teenagers, when Matt got Amy pregnant right before their high school graduation. Although Amy never gave birth, they had already moved in together and have been living with each other ever since."

"Matt rarely gives Amy a second thought at this point. He has basically forgotten all about her, and she is completely alone. Right now, she is almost entirely dependent on Matt's income, and she can't move back in with her parents. She is trapped where she is, and she feels that she has no choice but to stay with Matt and watch as he sleeps with numerous girls on the side. You need to help get her out of there."

"Unfortunately, I do not believe that there is any hope for Matt. He has been taken too far over and he lives in lust every day. There is very little that can be done for him at this point, although we may be able to help him further down the road. For now though, we will have to focus on getting Amy to a better place… I have been keeping an eye on the situation for some time now, trying to determine what the best option would be for her. I want you to bring her to Kyle, a man who lives in the same apartment building. Do what you can for her. Here is your leather satchel. I've added a few items for your quest. Take care."

Ladaya was much more abrupt in this encounter, trying to get rid of Valtina faster so that she didn't have any time to protest or ask questions. The less time she had to think over the mission, the better. So, as soon as she stopped speaking, Ladaya transported Valtina to Amy and Matt's apartment building.

Valtina traveled through space and time, watching the fog and mist disperse as she reached her destination. In the matter of only a few seconds, she had left Middle World and returned to Earth yet again. This time, she appeared in a dark alley in a neighborhood that must have been a lower class residential area. The worn brick of the apartment building next to her didn't seem trustworthy, and Valtina walked out from the alley toward the main road.

As she turned the corner, she saw a young man getting out of his car and jogging around the front of it. As he turned, he lost his balance and started to fall. After barely catching himself, he started laughing along with the girl in the passenger seat. They were both smiling as he opened the door for her and reached his hand out as an offering. She took it saying, "Thanks for the ride, Matt."

For a moment, Valtina was confused. She had automatically assumed that this man and woman were Matt and Amy, though it appeared she was only half correct. Seeing movement out of the corner of her eye, she saw a woman standing in an upstairs window, watching the scene taking place below. The sadness on her face was contagious and Valtina instantly sympathized with her. She left the window, turning away from her boyfriend. This was probably a smart choice because Matt leaned in and kissed the young woman as he pulled her from his car.

"Anytime, baby doll. You sure you don't want me to drive you the other block back to your apartment? Maybe I could stay for a while."

"Matt, I'm sure that your girlfriend is waiting for you already. You don't need to make me feel even guiltier!"

"She doesn't mind. It's not like we have any plans for tonight anyway."

"No Matt, thanks for the offer but I'll be fine walking… it's just a little bit further anyway." She turned and waved over her shoulder, walking away from him. She swayed her hips when she walked and he couldn't take his eyes off her ass.

"Hate to see you go, but love to watch you leave!" he called after her. Then he went inside, up the stairs to his apartment. Valtina followed close behind, despite her disgust at being so near him.

When they entered the apartment, it was easy to see that they didn't have a lot of money. It seemed most of this apartment was filled with cheap DIY furniture and cheap decorations. Although it was obvious that there wasn't a large budget for this home, it was also easy to see that a great deal of attention and consideration went into every aspect of the place. Valtina could feel Amy's energy coming from every direction. She was waiting on a bar stool at the kitchen counter as Valtina and Matt entered.

"Hey babe. How was work?"

"It was fine. Is dinner ready?" He walked over without glancing at her, picked up the plate of food that was set out for him, and took it to a recliner. He sat down, flipped on the TV, and took a bite of the food. He was served chicken and rice, and she automatically walked over to take out a cold beer from the refrigerator.

"Chicken's cold," he said gruffly.

"Sorry, I had it ready but you're a little later coming home than you usually are."

"Well, you can heat it up again."

She put the beer down on the counter, bowed her head, and took the plate. As she was doing this, Valtina removed a clear, colorless potion from the leather satchel and poured a few drops in the beer. After placing the plate in the microwave oven, Amy handed Matt the beer and returned to the kitchen. In a few minutes, Amy returned to Matt to serve the reheated chicken. She walked in a depressed manner, as though she was completely terrified of the man that she lived with. As she handed him the plate of food, she watched expectantly, waiting to see if he enjoyed it more this time around.

If you enjoyed this sample then look for **Unfaithful - The Leather Satchel Paranormal Romance Series, Book 2**.

Other Books by Darla Dunbar

- The Romeo Alpha BBW Paranormal Shifter Romance Series

- Romeo Alpha Blood Lines Romance

- The Alpha Feud BBW Paranormal Shifter Romance Series

- The Alpha Packed BBW Paranormal Shifter Romance Series

- The Mind Talker Paranormal Romance Series

- The Leather Satchel Paranormal Romance Series

Get the latest update on new releases from the author at:

https://darladunbar.com/newsletter/

About the Author - Darla Dunbar

Darla has been interested in paranormal romance since she was a teenager in high school. It was then that she discovered she could fulfill her fantasies through her writing.

Observing people and human behavior in the area of romance has always been one of her favorite pastimes. Combining that with an overactive imagination is a sure fire way of coming up with interesting themes.

Connect with Darla Dunbar

I really appreciate you reading my book! Here are my social media coordinates:

Friend me on Facebook: https://www.facebook.com/darladunbar/

Follow me on Twitter: https://twitter.com/DarlDunbar

Check me out on Goodreads: https://www.goodreads.com/author/show/8425857.Darla_Dunbar

Subscribe to my newsletter: https://darladunbar.com/newsletter/

Visit my website: https://darladunbar.com/

www.ingramcontent.com/pod-product-compliance
Lightning Source LLC
Chambersburg PA
CBHW030825200726
48288CB00004B/1399